The Kemetic Creation Story

DeBorah Marie

AuthorHouse™
1663 Liberty Drive
Bloomington, IN 47403
www.authorhouse.com
Phone: 1 (800) 839-8640

Published by AuthorHouse 11/09/2018

ISBN: 978-1-5462-6233-6 (sc)
ISBN: 978-1-5462-6234-3 (e)

The
Kemetic Creation
Story

DeBorah Marie

I am the ONE and the ALL,
I brought myself in to being.
I had all the power but
experience I was seeking.

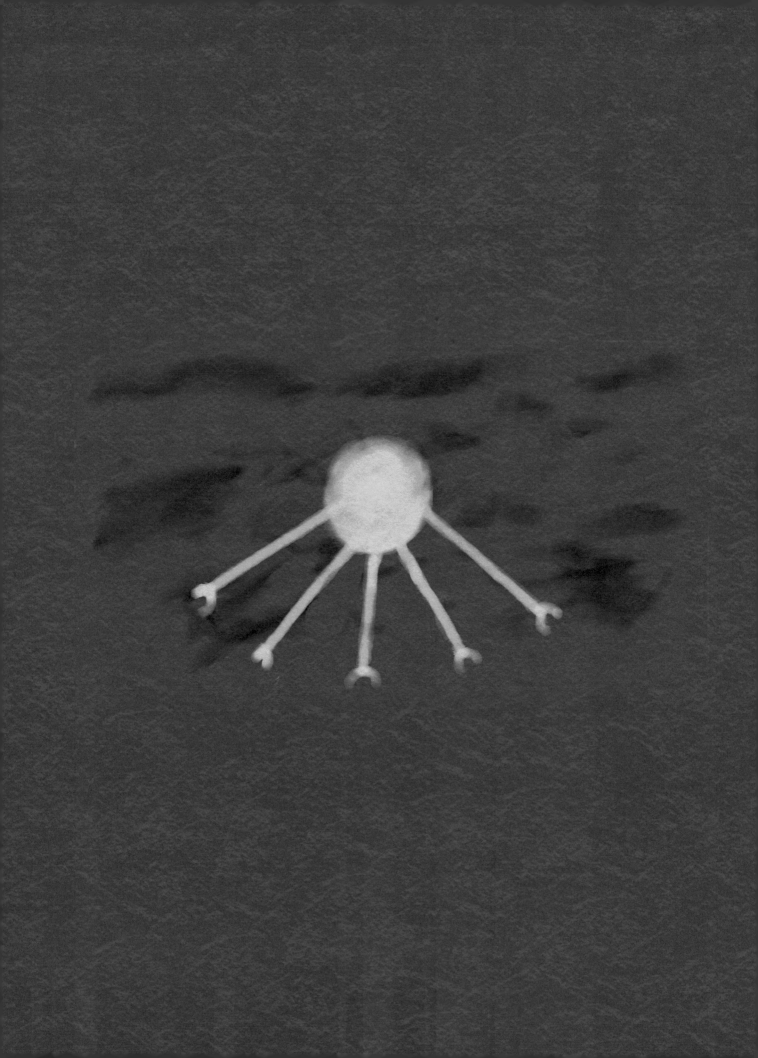

So first I create Nun, the
deep, dark, chaotic sea.
Then I rose from Nun and
created all that would be

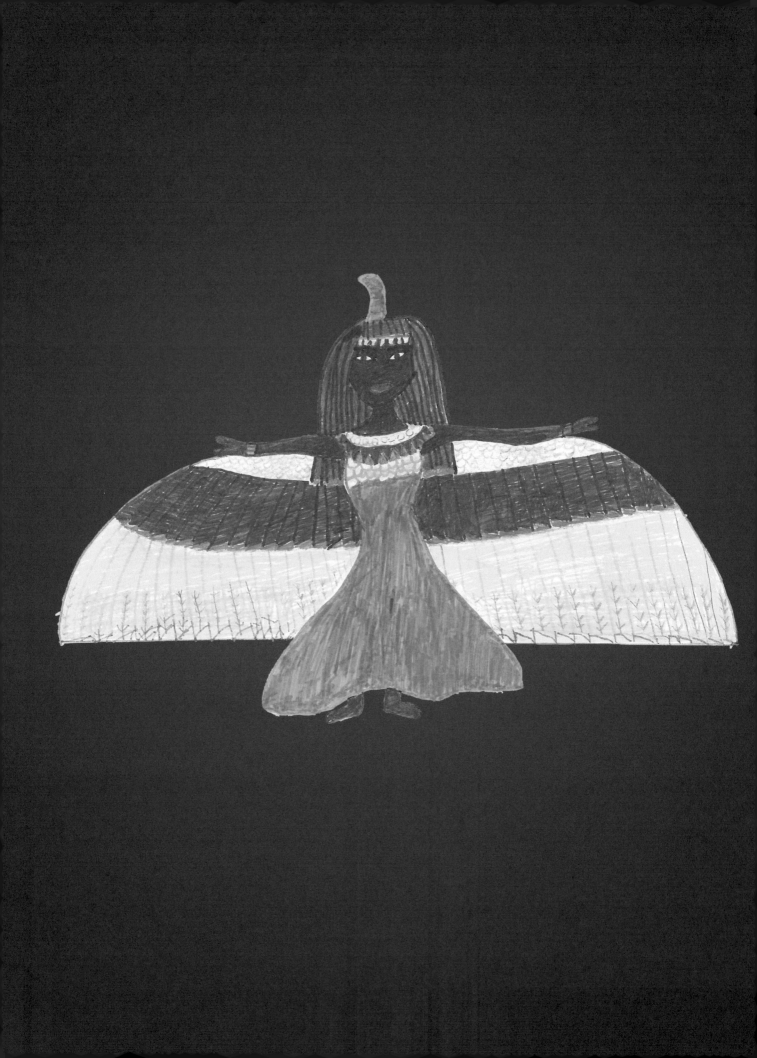

I created the goddess Maat,
to bring the world into order.

I created the god Djehuti

and the goddess Sesheta
to be the recorders.

I created the god Shu,
whose breath creates
the air that blows free

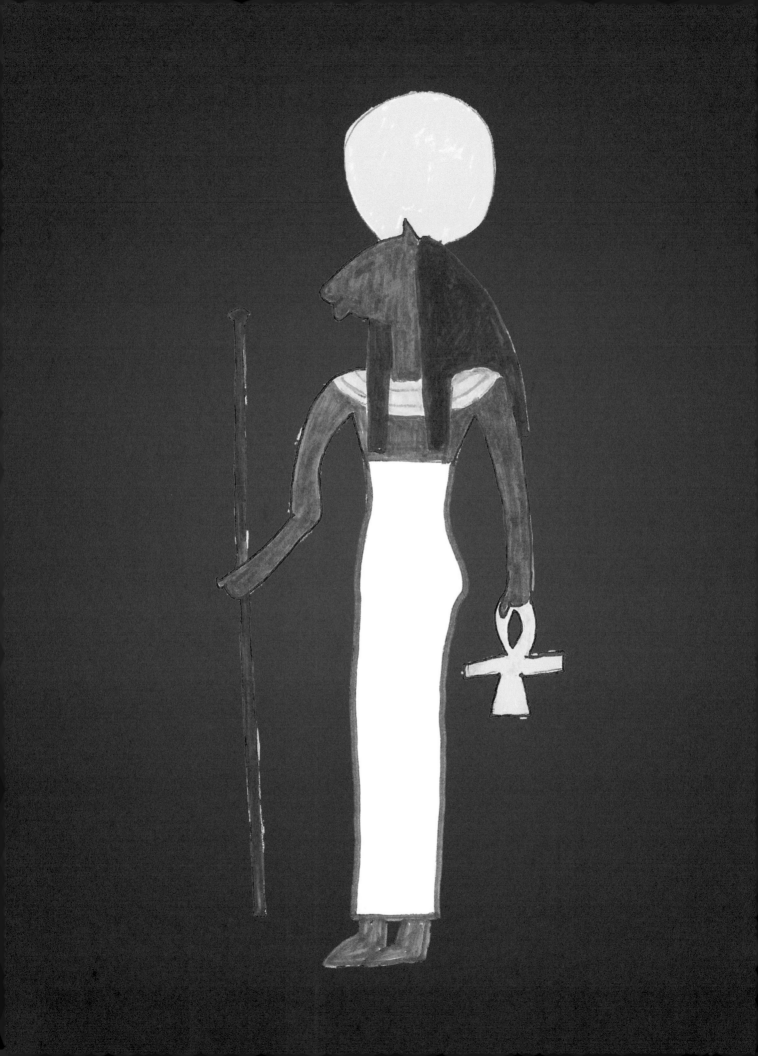

I created the goddess
Tefnut, whose tears
replenishes the sea.

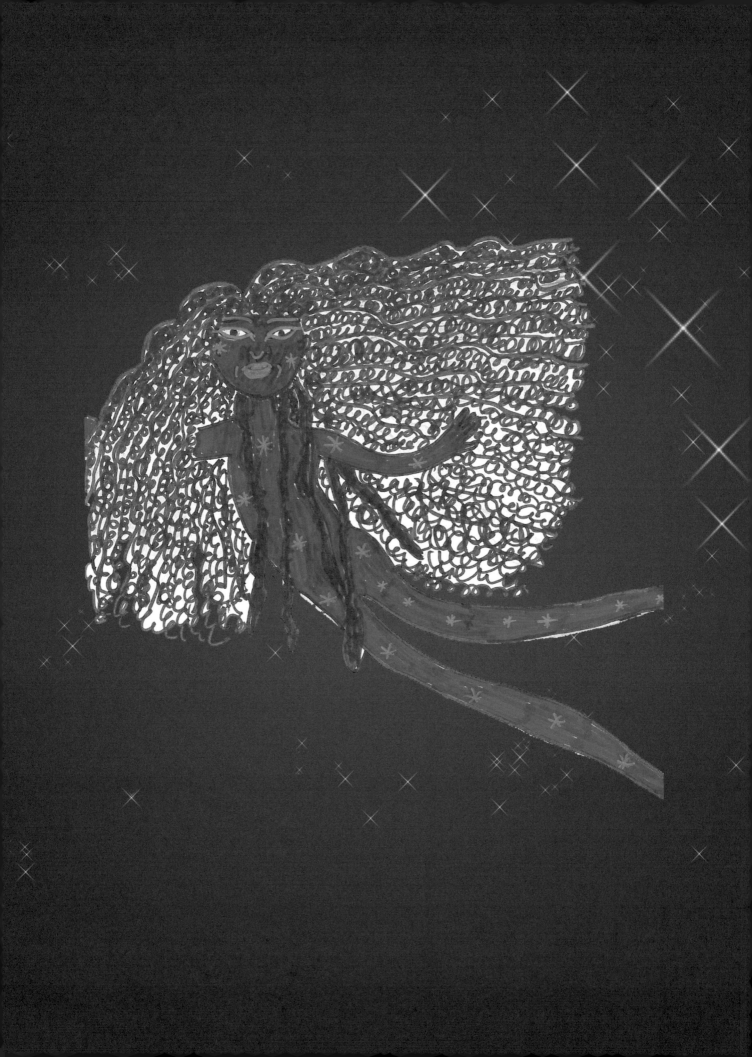

I created the goddess
Nüt, whose body holds
the planets and stars.

I created the god Geb,
whose body formed the
land here and far.

Then the sky goddess Nüt
and the earth god Geb
fell in love and marry,
and soon a flock of
babies Nüt shall carry.

First came Asar.

Followed by Set.

Then Nüt gave birth to
twins, Aset and Nebhet.

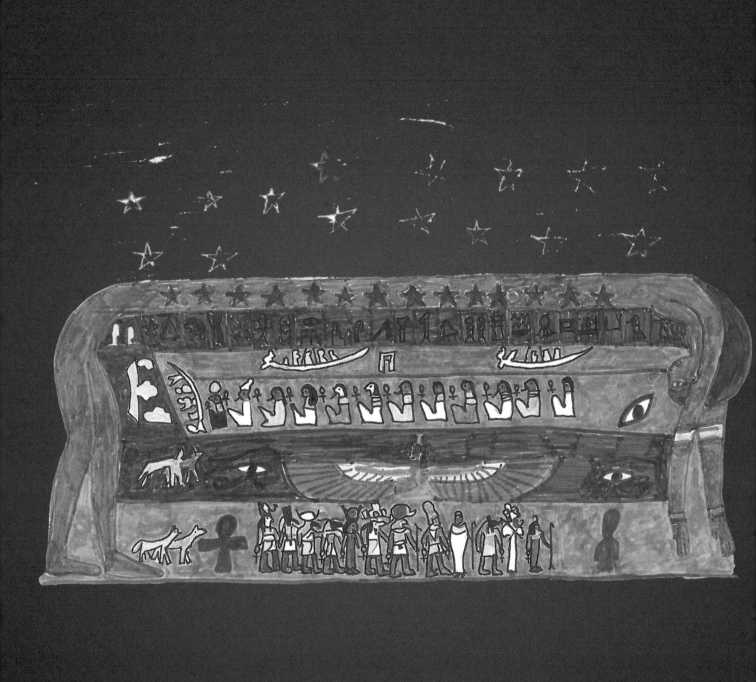

I saw what was created
and was filled with pride.

I was the mother and the
father of all far and wide.

Complete and perfect
in the land of plenty.
Out of the One
came the Many.

The Beginning.......

Printed in the United States
By Bookmasters